RED

ANNALEE ADAMS

RED

First edition. August 2023.

Copyright © 2023 Annalee Adams.

The moral rights of the author have been asserted.

Written by Annalee Adams.

This is a work of fiction. Similarities to real people, places, or events are entirely coincidental. All rights reserved.

ISBN: 9798 856 2125 86

This book has been typeset in Garamond.

www.AnnaleeAdams.biz

To their voices unheard, I hear you…

ANNALEE ADAMS

GRETEL

A BLOOD-CHILLING SERIAL KILLER SHORT STORY

Book One: Gretel.

Words have no power to impress the mind without the exquisite horror of their reality.

Edgar Allen Poe

1

Crimson blood circled my feet as I looked down at him. It wouldn't be long now. I'd often wondered how long it would take for a man to bleed out after I cut his penis off and fed to him. Now I had the chance to find out. Technically, though, I found out when I was thirteen years old. Well, I found out what a penis was, at least.

I was a delicate young thing, barely into my teenage years when they took me away from the life I once knew. Thrust into a nightmare of humiliation, isolation, and fear; subjected to unimaginable horrors, shared around like I was nothing, no one. There was no escape, no reprieve; I was powerless, another disposable soul lost to the darkness.

That was years ago. I sighed, wrapping my arms around myself. I can still remember when this asshole took me. The night was still and cold, the stars unseen behind a blanket of fog. He had found me hiding beneath the bed as his family murdered mine.

When I arrived at the mansion, I saw that the walls were decorated with golden frames filled with photos of young girls wearing pale pink dresses and a smile as fragile as porcelain. The air smelled sweet of tobacco and whisky; the scent only grew stronger when he gripped my arm and pressed his lips to mine. I recoiled away from him. No matter the lavish promises he made, or the gifts he bought, I only ever wanted to go home. I sighed, watching the contents of Stefan's stomach spew out all over his legs. The sight of which made me smile. Whenever I'd tried to leave, he'd restrain me. Now he's restrained. He'd wanted to try out his merchandise before he sold me to the highest bidder.

Shaking my head, I dug the dagger in deeper. Hyperventilating, he squeezed his eyes shut, crying out for forgiveness. He was my first time, the first man that touched me, down there. I hated every second of his stale breath as he puffed away, licking the sweat as it beaded on my forehead. Everything I am now is because of the pain I endured. The make-up, the dresses, expensive perfumes, they were all meant to transform me into a doll they could dress up and show off to their friends.

My youth quickly vanished under their hands, stealing away any sense of safety I had ever known. But now, it is my turn for vengeance. With each passing night, I can feel the wolves of the city slowly losing control over me. And as I look down into his frightened face, filled with regret and fear, he begs for mercy… but there is none. I have taken back what belongs to me: my innocence, my body, my life.

Warmth spread throughout my chest as I smiled and leaned down toward him, whispering, "I will never be your baby doll again, and neither will they." Salty tears mixed with blood, coating his chest, cleaning the canvas as I began, taking my time with every stroke of the blade, every swirling mark of the wolf. Caressing his chest with my blade, I marked him as the wolf he was, a predator in his prime. Smiling, I took my time, savouring every scream, every tear he wept for me. For if I didn't stop him now, those six girls huddled in the corner of the basement would lose everything they had and more.

Glancing over his shoulder, I could see the six young girls cowered in the cage. Two of the youngest were covering their eyes. Jesus, they were only five, possibly six at a stretch. Where were they taken from? I pursed my lips. I cannot recall any missing persons breaking news flashing across the TV last night. Taking a deep breath, I exhaled long and hard, weighed down by the realisation of it all.

I knew. These poor children were immigrants, bought over with their parents, seeking a new way of life. They never expected this, never asked for this.

A nearby hotel was being used to house immigrants, people fleeing the war-torn state abroad, as far as I knew. They were there for their safety, at least until they had arranged their papers. I had heard rumours, though; rumours of children being taken in their sleep; but I had never found it to be true until now. The sad part was, we ignored these people. The authorities didn't care. No one searched for them, they were undocumented. Perfect targets for the sleazy dark side of society.

I lifted my hand and drove the knife into his ball sack. The twisted piece of shit. How dare he take more innocent children and warp their minds with his sick pleasures? Half of these kids would have been sold. The other half, the ones that cried too much, would have been killed, buried in a mass grave somewhere.

Time passed quickly as I used my blade to carve the head of a wolf in his chest. By this time, he had stopped blubbering. Instead, he drifted in and out of consciousness. This must have been it. The time when the blood loss was too great, and he succumbed to his final breath. I'd never waited this long before with any of the others. Never had the patience. But he was special. He was my first Payne family member; and after seeing what he had done to the seventh girl whose body was decomposing in the corner, I had taken my time with him. Doing to him at least some of what he did to her. I looked over at her scattered body parts, wincing. It looked like he had taken his time with her breasts, carving them perfectly, like a surgeon performing a mastectomy. He had tossed those in the cage with the six young children. A warning perhaps. A warning that if they step out of line, this is what will happen to them. The thing is, I'm guessing most of those kids didn't even have breasts yet. But with the younger ones, well, they would never have survived the weekend antics they had put me through. They were too young, too... tight.

It sickens me now that this is what my life has come to. The thoughts that travel through my mind. The pain I once felt. It's all I know now. All I will ever know.

Looking down at the scumbag, I watched as his breathing slowed, heavy and distant. Each breath felt like an hour had passed by. His fingers had grown cold, his arms too. Body greying and breath seizing, and finally, just finally, he took his last breath, and I exhaled mine. I hadn't realised I'd been holding my breath, not until he died, withering before me. I was almost proud of the fact that the last thing he saw was my pale face. My deep brown eyes stared back at him with such malice. He had run his fingers over my cheekbones when he met me earlier tonight. Taking his time, promising me gifts he would never give, eager to take me back to his place and capture me for all time. What an asshole! Did he think I was that young, innocent girl I once was? Hell, he didn't even realise who I was!

He had met me as a child many years ago, and I was naïve enough to skip home alongside him. But not now. Not ever. Not after what I had seen and endured. Instead, I'd turned the tables. He was the first calling card I had ever left. The first brother, the eldest, and the first wolf of society I'd carved, and he would not be the last. Hell no, he would never be the last.

Wiping my blade on the remains of his trousers, I smiled. Relief took over me, flooding through me like a sense of sunshine and rainbows. One fewer wolf on the streets of a glorious city. One less victim to rescue or bury. Today was a good day.

Walking over to the cage, I smiled. "He's gone now, children. You're safe."

They still whimpered, huddled in the corner. I sighed. This entire ordeal would plague their every nightmare. I hope they will grow up to be happy, perhaps even protect others as I have. They need a life of unicorns and candyfloss, not of monsters of the night kidnapping children and selling them as sex slaves to the highest bidder.

I put my knife back in its sheath and took out my burner phone. It was handy working where I did. Josh and Kent would be on shift tonight and they're as slow as a sloth on his lunch break. I took a long, deep breath, wiped the beads of sweat from my forehead, and dialled the emergency services.

After leaving an anonymous tip, I released the children from the cage, explaining that help would soon be here. They nodded, huddled back together in the corner and watched me leave.

Turning away from them, I pulled up my red hood, hiding my deep auburn hair, and smiled to myself as I disappeared into the night. Tonight, I had taken the first of the Payne family, the first of many.

ANNALEE ADAMS - RED

2

The following morning, I awoke in my shabby apartment, staring up at the stained ceiling and wallpaper peeling on the far wall. It wasn't much, but this was home. Like always, it was cold from the broken heating system and single-floor heater. I'd lived here ever since I was sixteen, broken out of the trafficking trade by Detective Monroe, a dick of a police officer, but a friend nonetheless.

Monroe worked in homicide, and after he found me, he took me under his wing and became my closest friend; even though he was incredibly annoying and sometimes made the stupidest of decisions. But it was that one decision that saved my life that day.

On his day off, he'd followed a tip from a known druggie down on Old Saints Row. The addict informed him that several young girls were due to be sold on the black market. Monroe, being the curious cat he was, followed his nose and went in with zero backup. It still surprises me how he didn't get killed that day.

Apparently, he never caught sight of the main perpetrators, the Payne family, but he's been trying to put them behind bars ever since.

After the auction, things went quiet, and there was simply no evidence to pursue the case. After all, they usually wore masks when playing with all the girls… well, the living ones, at least.

That fiasco really shook things up at the station. Monroe took down the dick that was to be my new 'Daddy', the winning bidder, his partner, Chase Bernstein, and a detective he considered a long-time friend. That's when he found me and a handful of other girls huddled together in fear, covered in blood, but that's another story!

We were like little fish in a pond, moving around from one man to another. Each time we were owned by someone new; we returned to our puddle of friends where we felt safe again. Natasha was one of those fish; she was loud and bossy and glamorous. She was the eldest too, seventeen and getting too old for the creep we had to call Daddy.

Then there was me; the Baby Doll of the group, thirteen years old and pretty enough for my damnation. It meant they always chose me first and sold me to every sicko that wanted me next. I cannot count how many times they abused me like that. My body trembled at the thought. The best thing I've learnt to do is block it all out. The only thing that always plagues me is the bright white ceilings hanging down low with large posts holding them up. They all had beautiful chandeliers that I eyed as the mattress moved up and down, while the man above me took every advantage, abusing me in any way he could think of; using every part of my body until he grew tired and then throwing me into a corner to lick my wounds alone.

Those ceilings were my only escape back then, my soul escaping into the cleanliness for a while. But now, those clean, crisp white edges only reminded me of their heavy weight crashing down on me year after year; those sweaty hands holding down my head and neck as I screamed and struggled beneath them. Sobbing my little heart out, they continued until they had finished what they started, throwing me aside like a rag doll with nothing left inside. Those clean, crisp white edges only remind me of how deathly cold they were against my bruised neck, how blinding they were when my tears stung my eyes in the dark; begging silently; No more... no more please... those innocent words falling on deaf ears through thin walls. I will never be that scared young girl again. I buried her deep in my soul.

So now I'm a junior detective, looked after by the dick that is Monroe, the old detective with an attitude problem, but a big heart. He had pushed me up the ladder himself. Said I needed to feed all that anger into something, so I did. I help people in more ways than one. But he will never know that side of me. Although I sometimes wonder if he suspects.

The phone rang, and I edged up the bed, checking my surroundings. Home.

"Hello"

"Red, it's Monroe." He had called me Red ever since he saved me, I'm guessing because I never uttered my real name, too afraid to be that naïve baby doll again.

"Yeah, it's six in the morning, Monroe, and my day off. What do you want?"

He laughed. "There's no such thing as a day off in the police force, sweet pea."

I growled. "Red I can withstand, but sweat pea, come on, when have you ever known me to be sweet?"

The old guy laughed some more. "Well, there's been another vigilante killing."

"Ooo now, why didn't you start with that?"

"Well, I thought we'd have an actual conversation first."

"Where?"

"Down on Pennytram Avenue."

"I'll be fifteen."

"Better make it ten. I'm in the car outside."

I walked over and looked out of the window. Three storeys down there was his old green Volvo, waiting for me.

Heading over to the chest of drawers, I pulled out an old band tee shirt and black jeans. Washing and dressing quickly, I threw back my hair into a messy bun and grabbed my dark red hooded coat, badge, and gun. Screw dressing in suits. I wasn't one of them and never would be.

Monroe was standing smoking outside. I shuddered. He noticed and put it out. "Sorry, love, I'm still trying to quit."

Nodding, I got in the passenger seat and waited for him to join me.

As he got in, he hacked out a cough. His grey roots shone through the mat of brown hair, lit by the early morning sun. He needed it dying again, still trying to act like he was thirty years younger than he was.

"So, what's the background?" I asked. He turned around and smirked.

"First, what are you wearing? You do realise that your top is covered in swear words." I hadn't. But I wasn't going to own up to the fact.

"It's fashion, apparently."

"Since when are you fashionable?" he tutted and dug around in the grubby back seat behind him. "Here, wear this." He held up a plain white tee shirt. I scowled at him. "What? It's Masie's!"

"Look, I'm not knocking your daughter's taste, but why do you have a spare set of her clothes in here?"

He narrowed his eyes. "You know she gets travel sick." Yes. Yes, I knew that.

"Ah yes, I still remember when she threw up all over me after that Indian we went to."

He smirked. "Now change!"

"I can't wear that. I'm wearing a black bra."

"So…"

"It'll show through."

"Look Red, a black bra is nothing compared to whatever that is you're wearing!"

Smirking, I nodded, and he turned away. I changed quickly, throwing my tee shirt onto the back seat.

"Much better."

I scowled. "Can we go then!"

Starting the engine, we drove to Pennytram Avenue, the scene of my latest crime. Not that ridding the world of scumbags like that asshole was a crime in my book. Vigilante or not, I was doing the world a favour.

"So, the victim is male, mid-thirties, white, with a carved wolf's head on his chest."

I had to stop myself from smiling at that and nodded instead. "He's one of the Payne's known traffickers from the East side."

"Well, they're a bunch of assholes. He probably deserved it."

"Shush," he said, then smirked. "You know I agree, especially with what you went through, but we have to uphold the law, not applaud those who break it."

The rest of the journey was silent.

ANNALEE ADAMS - RED

3

We arrived at the scene quickly. I couldn't help but smile to myself, knowing I would come face to face with his rotting corpse. Although I had to stay quiet, I couldn't give the game away this early, could I?

We pulled up outside the scene. Monroe got out first and greeted the forensics team. As he checked on a few details, I entered and walked around the body, admiring my work. Now I was never that good at drawing. Hell, I had failed my art exam the day I'd taken it, but this wolf looked damned brilliant, almost like it was trying to escape out of his chest. Maybe that's it, maybe a pen and paper were never the tools I should have worked with. Because if this was my art piece for the exam, I'd bloody ace it this time!

As usual, I pretended to search for clues about who the killer could be, and my stomach dropped as I caught sight of a necklace, a necklace right beside Monroe's feet. My bloody necklace! And not only that, it was one that Monroe and his wife Esme gave to me the Christmas before last. God damn it! Shaking my head, I bent down, trailing over the body, eyeing the floor and pretending to tie my shoe. Okay, so I can't do that. I don't have laces. Bloody boots! Okay, so back to the old tactics.

"Monroe, what's that?" I said, pointing at the cage where the kids had been.

"Jeez, Louise! Was that where they were kept he said?" Looking over at it, and away from the necklace.

I walked over, fake tripped over, landing by his feet, popping the necklace into my hand, then pocket.

"What the…" he laughed, helping me up. The forensics team was shaking their heads as I disturbed the scene. They were getting used to me doing that, though. "You need to watch where you're going, kid."

"You think!" Crisis averted!

"Who?"

"What?"

"Who was kept in there? You said someone was in there?"

He raised his eyebrows and sighed. "Kids, six of them."

"All alive?"

He nodded. "Yeah. We had an anonymous tip. Whoever it was, they saved those girls."

"What about the body?"

"Well, they sure didn't like him!" he smirked.

"Oh, now… you're allowed to smirk about the dead guy and I'm not?"

He coughed. "Ahem, no you're not."

"Aren't you glad he's dead?"

"After what he did to the seventh girl. Yeah, I damned well am."

I smiled. He was coming around. "But that doesn't mean whoever did this did the right thing. The murderer committed a crime and should be bought to justice for it." Well, damn. I nodded, feigning my understanding.

Harves walked over with his long beard greying by the second. I smirked. I'm not sure which one's older, Monroe or Harves.

"So what do you make of this?" he asked Monroe, ignoring me. After all, I was still a junior detective… to him, it meant I knew nothing.

Monroe turned to me. "What do you think, Red?"

I smiled, secretly thanking him. "Well, the perp had a motive. The victim was connected to a known criminal organisation, so it's possible that this was retaliation or a warning from a rival gang. The fact that we found the kids alive could suggest that the killer had a moral compass, or at least didn't want to harm innocent civilians."

Harves stroked his beard, nodding in agreement. "It's a good theory. We'll have to look into the victim's connections and see if any of them match up with our suspect list."

I tried my best to hide my excitement. This was the closest I had ever been to getting caught, and yet they were considering my theory as a serious lead. I had to tread carefully from here on out.

Monroe clapped his hands. "Alright, let's wrap this up. I want to see if I can get anything from the security cameras in the area. Red, why don't you inspect the carved wolf and see if you can find any significance behind it?"

I nodded, trying not to show the joy bubbling up inside of me. As they walked away, I checked my pocket to make sure the necklace was still there. It was. I shook my head and closed my eyes for a moment, sighing with relief. I couldn't believe how careless I had been, leaving behind something that could connect me to the crime!

As I examined the wolf tattoo on the victim's chest, I took a deep breath and smiled. I couldn't help but feel a sense of pride, my thoughts consumed by my success. At this rate, the rest of the traffickers won't know what's coming! I felt the urge to trace my gloved finger along the carved lines on Stefan Payne's bare, bloodied chest. It even looked like a wolf! This was my art, my way of leaving my mark on the world, and a warning to all those that worked with this family. And… as long as I was careful, I knew they would never catch me. But the thrill of the chase, the rush of adrenaline, it was all worth it. I was doing the world a favour, one victim at a time.

"I don't think you should touch him!" Monroe said, his eyes narrowed.

I smiled. "It's good, don't you think?"

He eyed Stefan's chest, pursed his lips and nodded. "Yes, so, we're looking for some kind of artist?" he asked, testing my skills.

"Err, yes, I guess so. I mean, they must be if they can carve this."

"What do you think it was carved with?"

I took a moment before answering this. I knew the answer, but I had to answer it with what I could see, not what I knew when I'd been there. "Something extremely sharp."

"What makes you say that?"

"The carved lines are narrow but deep, therefore it must be some kind of blade."

He nodded. "You're getting good at this."

I smiled, then gulped.

"Right," Harves said, walking over. "There was a homeless man three doors down. I'm going to get a deputy to take his statement, then head back to the station." Well shit…

"Anything on the cameras?" he asked.

Monroe huffed. "No, they were all smashed from another angle, bloody useless."

"Damn!"

"Yeah, damn," I said, shaking my head. God, I'm good. Harves shook his head at me and walked off. Monroe smirked.

"He doesn't like me much, does he?" I asked, smirking.

He laughed. "He doesn't like many people."

"He likes you."

"He tolerates me."

I laughed. "Fair point."

"So, breakfast then?"

I nodded. "Totally, I'm starving!"

4

A rickety bell dinged as I pushed open the door to the greasy spoon cafe. A place Monroe and I frequented when we were on a case over this side of the city. Old grease coated my hand and the familiar scent of sizzling bacon caressed my senses, topped off by the aroma of freshly brewed coffee. Georgia waved from the corner; she was dressed in her usual yellow-stained waitress uniform, with her breasts popping out of the top. The burly woman came bounding over, eager to take our order.

"Usual table?" she asked. Monroe nodded.

We sat down at the worn wooden table and she pulled out her dirty ragged cloth to mop up the old coffee stain on the plastic cover; right by where I was sitting down. I smiled; the state of this place provided me with some comfort.

To the side was a menu with tattered corners, not that we needed it. We knew everything by heart. Next to that sat the half-empty sugar dispenser, the ketchup and brown sauce containers, coated with remnants of whoever used it last.

Georgia poured us both a cup of black coffee and took our orders, an old English fry-up with extra bacon. She smiled and walked off to greet the next customers as the door's bell dinged.

I sat staring at the familiar faded wallpaper as Monroe filled his cup with sugar. He smiled as I turned and watched him. "That stuff will kill you, you know," I said.

He laughed. "I think I'm old enough to know that by now, Red."

"Exactly," I smirked. "You're old enough to know better."

His brow furrowed, and he pouted. I swear if there weren't people around, he would have stuck out his tongue at me. Sometimes I wonder who's the adult here. Age has nothing to do with it.

He pulled out his notebook.

"So… what do you think, kid?"

"Kid… really?"

He laughed again, slurping his coffee.

I pursed my lips, tapping my fingers on the table. "Okay so, we know he had something to do with kids." Monroe nodded. "What happened to them, anyway?"

"They were taken to St Oswald Hospital to get the all-clear. Uniform is tracking their parents down at present, but they are finding it difficult as they don't speak English."

"Isn't Marge in?" Marge was our on-call translator and a long-time friend of the family. He shook his head. Bugger, I would have liked to know what they were going to say. Did I mentally scar them more than that sicko Stefan did?"

I absentmindedly rubbed the tight muscles in the back of my neck as I went over my options. "What about Joey, the sketch artist?"

My stomach turned, and my heart raced at the thought, But I had to suggest it. They'd use Joey, anyway.

Then, inspiration struck; perhaps a mask was the solution for the future. I pictured the form-fitting tie masks with eyeholes. It could work, but then again, it would be so inconvenient! No, I wanted those bastards to see my face before they died. It had to be the last thing that they ever saw.

"We have bought Joey in. Once the girls have been checked out, and social finally turns up." He yawned. "He'll get started." I nodded, silently peeing myself... metaphorically speaking.

Georgia turned up with two full plates of yummy goodness. Bacon, tomatoes, black pudding, greasy sausages, beans, fried bread, two runny eggs and more bacon! I licked my lips. I was in heaven!

"You'll turn into me one day if you eat all of that."

I raised my eyebrows. "Neh, you're big enough for the both of us."

He grinned. "I don't know where you put it all."

I winked and took the first mouthwatering bite. It was a sensation of salty, sweet, and smoky, coated with the runny yolk of an egg, satisfying the hunger pangs I'd had all morning.

Monroe's phone rang. He answered, mumbled a few things, then ended the call.

"So?" I said, eager to know who it was.

He smiled. "It was Harves. He said the witness is homeless and stunk of old whisky."

"Oh," I said, trying to sound disheartened. Thank fuck though! Whatever he says won't stand up in court. "Did he see anything?"

"Yes, well no actually, he heard screams."

"Ah, that must have been the victim. Didn't he see who else was there?"

"No, apparently he couldn't see very well due to the copious amounts of alcohol he had consumed that day."

"Oh… that's a shame," I said, pinching myself to stop me grinning. He nodded, then continued to eat.

I took another mouthwatering bite, glimpsing the bacon on my fork before it entered my mouth. Wrinkled. It was so wrinkled. It reminded me of the hands of the old man I once called Daddy; the vile leader of the pack, the man with the broken heart tattoo. I placed the forkful down and shuddered. I wanted no memory of that man inside of me ever again, not him, nor his offspring.

"Everything alright?" Monroe said, frowning.

"Huh?" I blinked a few times and brought myself back to reality. "Yeah, I've eaten too much. Couldn't manage that last bite."

He laughed, emptying his plate.

I turned away, watching a young couple outside. They seemed so… happy, carefree, almost. I sighed. If only life could be like that for me.

When he finished, he sat back, full to the brim, watching as I slurped my coffee.

"You're tired, aren't you?" he asked, brows furrowed and stating the bloody obvious.

I smiled. "Is it that obvious?" He nodded.

Georgia came over to the table and took away the plates, topping our coffees up. "So, what do you think about the case?" I asked Monroe.

He paused, looked at me, and smiled. "I think whoever did this knew what they were doing. The murder was passionate, and the perp took their time. They wanted him to suffer. So, I'd say we need to investigate the victim's past relationships… a jilted lover, perhaps?" I nodded. "No… that's not quite it."

I frowned. "What do you mean?"

"The children, they had something to do with this."

"What about the parents?" I asked, feeling bad at pointing the blame towards innocent civilians.

"Could be. But this wasn't anger. If someone solely murdered him due to anger, then it would have been brutal, but also quick. This lasted hours."

"How can you tell?" I asked, stifling a yawn.

"The wolf you investigated. That would have taken time to carve."

"Hmm, that's a fair point. So, who then?"

He looked at me, really looked, then said, "I don't know... yet." What does he mean by that? Why the pause, why the glued expression? Does he know? Does he know it's me? I bit my lip, palms clammy. Taking a deep breath, I feigned a smile, wiping my palms on the seat. Shit. I cannot deal with this now. I have barely begun. I stifled another yawn, trying to keep my composure.

"Come on, let's get you home. You're worn out!" I nodded, finishing my coffee. "I take it the sleeping tablets aren't helping?"

I exhaled quickly. "No, they just trap me in the damn nightmares."

He slowly shook his head and stood up. "Ready to go?" I nodded, stood up and left the money on the table for breakfast.

Following Monroe, I got in the car and we left; he was lost in thought. I too eased myself into the silence of the journey. If he knows, wouldn't he say? Perhaps my mind is playing tricks on me. Maybe he doesn't know? I sighed, squashing myself further into the seat, closing my eyes and listening to the silence as he drove me home.

"Wakey, wakey!" Monroe yelled, catching me in a slumber. Fearful of the unknown, I shot up, restrained by my seat belt, fear strangling me until I realised where I was and who I was with.

"Ah, bad dream?" he said as I narrowed my eyes. "We're here rookie!"

I smirked, "enough of the rookie!" I said as I slammed the old car door shut, running inside to escape the rain.

"Hey Red," he yelled from the wound-down window. "Don't forget it's Taco Tuesday tonight. You know you're always welcome. Maisie would love to see you."

I groaned. I hated letting them down, but I had to free the city of these vile beings before another girl gets hurt.

"Neh, I'm beat. Need to catch up on some well-earned kip."

He laughed. "All you young ones ever do is sleep!" He shook his head. "So, tomorrow maybe?" I smiled and nodded. I doubt tomorrow would be good either, but I cannot exactly tell him why. God, I wish I could. Keeping these secrets from him, from Maisie… it is grinding me down, tearing away my heart and soul piece by piece. Eventually, I won't survive this.

Watching him go, the looming dread of those four words flickered through my mind. 'I don't know yet.' Is he using me to collect more evidence? Evidence on the murderer... on me? I huffed, shaking my head. He wouldn't. He knows it would destroy me. Monroe's been like a father to me. The real father type, not like the times I had to call 'them' Daddy. That was a whole other story.

Entering my home was a sigh of relief. Tears welled in my eyes. It was hard, so damn hard, to keep up this front. I wanted to scream, shout, and strangle every fucking asshole in this city. The anger and the pain screeched through me, boiling my blood and igniting my soul. There was something deep and deadly inside of me now. There had been ever since I left that god-forsaken place. I went in such a sweet, innocent, although reckless and naïve teenager, and I came out broken, battered, and abused. I was beyond repair, and there was not enough duct tape in the world to hold me together.

Monroe had suggested counselling after he'd found me. I tried it. But I could never truly open up to them. What I had gone through, no councillor could ever understand. No one can understand, except the brothers that sold and raped me repeatedly. They heard my screams; they owned my body, and no matter how hard I fought, they never gave up restraining me, pushing me.

It was the monster that owned me that I despised the most. The Payne's brother's father. He was the head of the family. The mastermind behind the whole operation. I had never seen his face. He was always in shadow, masked, or behind a screen. Bile swirled in my stomach, threatening to explode out of me like a washing machine in a spin cycle. I took a deep breath, calming my body one limb at a time.

I still remember his fucked up robotic voice. He'd said I had a fire in my eyes, and that he saw himself in me. The last time I ever saw that masked monster, he pulled away the voice changer, gripped me tight, and told me he loved me. How fucked up is that? I was sixteen, sixteen at the time! He must have been at least fifty!

If being his Baby Doll wasn't bad enough, it was when he said that no matter where I am, who I'm with, or what I'm doing, he will always be watching and listening. He said he owned me, now and always, whether I wanted him to or not. I can never be rid of the father, the true Daddy, not until the day I die… or he does.

For the rest of the day, I seethed. Anger burning through me, my past destroying me. The darkness was getting closer. I could feel it. Almost as much as I could feel my skin crawl as insects burrowed their way deep into my soul, ravaging it, leaving it in the darkness. Breathing in the memories of where I'll always live, now and always, that young broken girl.

ANNALEE ADAMS - RED

5

The night was a cold one. I wrapped myself up in my long red coat, hood up, head down. I'd learned where most of the cameras were over this side of the city, especially as this was where they bought and sold most of the children.

Walking the streets alone was a stupid idea for any female, any female except me, of course. After Monroe found me, I'd taken to training. Not just training with the police force, but training how to fight, how to wield the daggers I now used to take the lives of the scum of this city. It had taken years, but I needed to channel my anger into something, and cleansing this city was my only purpose; if I relied on the law, I would be no closer to taking down the Payne family business than when I started.

I'd discovered in the past year that the head of the Payne family was responsible. He was the one that paid out for the innocent to be taken. Paying for them to be filmed, raped, abused, and murdered, all while they watched in his sick, pathetic room, away from any prying eyes. He was the coward behind the screen… always was, and always would be.

My sources had told me that Xander was home. He was one of the three sons of the top man himself. Even to think of him made me shiver. Daddy dearest was always the one who caressed me after every ordeal and held me when I sobbed my little heart out. I can still remember the broken heart tattoo on his hand, faded and wrinkled.

Daddy Payne had no face, no original voice, and no real name, at least not a name I'd been able to find out. So, if Xander was back, and seen on the streets near the hotel that housed the undocumented children, I can guarantee that's more kids being taken. I only hope I can get there in time.

So, I took a trip back to the point of my captivity, the last place they'd taken me. Monroe wouldn't tell me where it was, and they had locked the police records in the basement evidence rooms. This left little information to be discovered about my abduction. I had leaned on friends and contacts, to no avail. So, I used my God-given talent for murder and whittled the information out of Stefan. It is laughable how talkative a man can be when you have their balls teetering under a blade, execution style.

Exploring the outer parts of the city, I found it. An exquisite yet secretive mansion. The place had recently become active again after they found its previous owner, Robert Payne, murdered and butchered by children. I hold my hand up to that one. I was one of them. He was the uncle to the dear old dead guy on Pennytram Avenue.

Back then, there were a lot of us girls; some made it, some didn't. You could tell the ones that would survive the day they tied them to that vile bed. If they screamed too much, it turned into a snuff video with eyes popping, brains smashed and slow knife wounds letting them bleed out. The whole thing terrified me, even now. The thought of going back inside makes my skin crawl.

I took a deep breath, staring at the tall white building before me. Fear crept up my backbone, clasping its tendrils around my chest, making it hard to breathe. It was a house of horrors. A place is only good for the sorrow and torment of little girls. I'd cried myself to sleep many nights, wondering if tomorrow would be my last day.

Climbing over the wall, my heart beat faster, my legs weakening by the minute. I was right to be afraid. I needed to be on alert.

Jumping down, I landed on the muddy ground, sheltered by trees; already cursing the fact I was unprepared for what I could hear approaching me.

I should have known it would have been guarded, after all the Payne's were cowards, hiding behind their cameras. The thundering of four legs ran towards me. Guard dogs. Not just one, but a pack of them. Snarling, salivating guard dogs. Well, shit. Grabbing the nearest stick, I waved it before them. "Here doggy doggy, do you like to play fetch?" I said, my voice quivering. Taking a deep breath, the only thing I could do in this instance was RUN!

Adrenaline surged, and every breath I took was fast and quivering. I was only about thirty feet from the entrance. I could make it. Or so I thought. Pounding feet echoed through the night and I drew my daggers, just in case. I didn't want to kill the beasts; I was an animal lover, after all. But these hounds were no longer the fluffy house pets I knew and loved. These creatures were dark, nasty, gnashing, drooling murderers in the making, and I was their next meal.

The growls of the approaching pack of dogs grew louder as they got closer, their eyes dark and wild. Their leader broke into a run and lunged for me, his teeth catching on my calf and ripping through the fabric of my trousers, sending a searing pain radiating up my leg. I screamed in terror, with my hand on my mouth, trying to quieten the cries.

Staggering my way to the side entrance, I saw the chain and lock holding it hostage. All I could do was cling to the daggers in each hand and try to keep the beasts away with wild swipes as I sliced and diced at the air like a madwoman. The dogs watched, growling but staying back.

With wild eyes, I searched for another way in. Then, to my relief, I noticed the window at the side of the building was open. Finally, some good luck! Taking a deep breath, I edged forwards, battling the hounds with the daggers, thrashing at the air like my life depended on it. Although I had the feeling, it did!

Shuffling over the stone pavement, blood trailing behind me. The dogs followed, snarling, their heated breath puffing into the midnight air. Claws scraping the stone growls igniting the air with their fury. I bit my lip, bracing against the pain in my leg as I hauled myself inside. Tears streaming down, I picked myself up off the ground, lent upward and gripped the cold metal handle, slamming the window shut.

Collapsing back on the floor, I clasped one hand over my bite, as the other clamped to my chest. It fucking hurts! No matter how hard I brace myself against the pain, I was an injured fish swimming in a sea of sharks. I wasn't getting out of this one alive.

Taking a few minutes to recall the shitty breathing exercises the counsellor had taught me. I took a deep breath, slowing down my breathing, calming myself and gaining control again. Slowly but surely, the world righted itself again and everything came back into focus.

I was in the dining room, and I only hoped I didn't bleed out before I had the chance to end that asshole's life. Taking a deep breath, the scent of old wood choked back in my throat, battling against a pungent floral perfume, just like the one they made me wear.

A large mahogany table stood above me. Velveteen curtains hung on the cream walls, decorating the room with large brocade patterns.

At the head of the table, a chandelier hung from the ceiling, full of crystals, sparkling like the stars on a storm-free night. I shuddered, exhaling slowly. This place… it was too clean, too vibrant, almost. I couldn't stand the perfection of it all.

Biting my lower lip, I looked down at my wound. It was a nasty bite, but nothing that would kill me quickly, at least not if I dressed it quickly enough.

Blood pooled around me, soaking through my clothes and spreading over the cream carpet. I was starting to feel the effects of blood loss, swaying, steadying myself against the wall. Grabbing the drape beside me, I used my dagger to slice a long piece off, wrapping it around my leg, and applying pressure to slow the steady flow of blood. It was a bloody good job that the dog didn't hit an artery, else I'd be toast!

Taking a few minutes, I began to recover. Luckily, I had planned for shit to hit the fan, and pulled out a bottle of water, which I gulped down; and my first aid kit, which I used to help me pin the makeshift bandage in place. Next, I took out a bottle of bleach, which I then used to cover my bloodstain on the carpet. There. My job, along with all the CSI programs I watched, was paying off!

As time passed, the dizziness eased. Taking a deep breath, I braced for the pain, stood up, and exhaled. It didn't hurt as bad as I thought it would.

But then again, a few gulps of the finest whisky I found on the shelf by the table helped.

Now, I was on a mission and I wouldn't let anything stand in my way, so I left the room, watching out for more guard dogs, just in case. On the inside, I could see that the place was well-maintained. The Payne's must have employed maids. There wasn't a speck of dust anywhere.

I quickly made my way through the corridors of the mansion, keeping to the shadows. It wasn't long before I found myself directly outside the door of the main suite.

It was now or never. He had to be in there, tormenting innocent children with his sadistic fetishes. I squared my shoulders and took a deep breath before opening the door and entering the room. It was dark, and Xander stood in the centre, watching the children cry before him. One girl was down on her knees, sobbing.

My hands gripped the daggers. I inched closer to him, trying not to make a sound as I crossed the room. But I was too slow. He must have sensed my presence, as he spun around. I gulped back bile as I came face to face with the second son, the middle child, Xander Payne. His face was full of both rage and confusion at being caught in the act.

He kicked the girl over, and she cried out. Then he laughed, staring at me. Raising my daggers, I stepped toward him, and instead of tackling me like he used to, he ran out of the side door. Bloody coward.

"Stay there!" I yelled, running after him.

I chased him through the mansion, pain eviscerating through my body, igniting every nerve, every electrical impulse. Blood loss was getting to me and no matter how quick I hobbled on, he would outrun me ten times over. I huffed, panting through the agonising humiliation of it all.

He was laughing as he skipped around me, clearly enjoying the race. "It's nice to see you've come home, Baby Doll."

I growled, angry, filled with hatred. He was one of many that deserved a long painful death.

Eventually, he ran into my last captor's bedroom, his uncle; the one the girls and I murdered; right before we were beaten black and blue and taken to the auction where Monroe found us.

That's when I saw it, all laid out there for the taking. The evidence I needed to take down the Payne family business. Photographs, videos, and documentation of their wrongdoing. He laughed some more as I walked towards him. "Now what are you going to do with those, Baby Doll? Didn't your mother never teach you not to play with knives?"

"Stop calling me Baby Doll!" I yelled, anger boiling in my blood. He laughed some more.

"Oh, Father would be so proud of the killer you've become. It's almost like you're a Payne yourself."

I stopped, taken aback. Wait. Was I as bad as he was? My forehead furrowed, and as I doubted myself, I gave him just enough time to grab a vase and smash me over the head with it.

Darkness.

6

Well, that all turned into a shit show! These were the first words I thought of when I awoke with a pounding headache, sporting a lump the size of Mount Everest.

Slithers of light penetrated my vision as my eyelids flickered open.

At the back of the room, Xander was playing with camera lighting. I shuddered as snippets of my past flickered through my mind. Flashlights always intensified everything. They made you so hot, sweat running from your body in a wild panic. The metallic tang of fear hit the back of my throat. I was back here again, back in my worst nightmare, tied up, stripped bare and being filmed for their pleasure. The memory was like a puppet show; an illusion, a story so bold, so tragic, it could and should never be told. My life until now was one of desperation, clumsily scratching at the darkness of my mind, pleading for a way out. I had been rescued from this place before, but my mind had never left there. I would always be that girl, tied to this bed, exposed, and abused repeatedly.

I don't know how long I'd been out. But it had been long enough for him to set up a studio in what appeared to be his bedroom. He had a tripod with a state-of-the-art camera, and a built-in mirror on the far wall -which at guess was a reciprocal one-way mirror.

Biting my lower lip, I pulled on the ropes. He had tied hands and feet to each of the bedposts. The sick fuck. I wanted to bleach my body for even being in his presence, let alone with what I knew was coming next.

He laughed to himself as he took a few pictures on his phone, getting up close and personal. I began edging away as much as possible until I realised it only made me look like the victim. My blood boiled at the thought of it. I would never be his victim again! Somehow, I know I will get out of this and I will take my time carving every inch of his chest into the wolf that he is. Every scream he makes will only make me carve deeper. Every time he pleads for forgiveness, I will laugh at his sadistic face. I will come out of this unscathed, I will save those poor children, and I will be one step closer to taking down the Kingpin of them all, Daddy dearest.

Xander disappeared behind the studio lighting again. I watched him. But something nagged at me. My gut was telling me this didn't feel right. I wasn't his usual type. I'm too old for any of his sex films. Where's the money in that? So, what was he planning?

Metaphorically scratching my head, I thought for a moment while looking around the room. At the end of the bed, there was a vibrant chaise lounge, covered in all manner of bondage gear and oh shit! My eyes widened. There was a sparkling, shimmering, delightful selection of knives, positioned neatly next to one another. Laid out next to them was the suffocation option, a see-through plastic bag. Beside those was a noose, an axe, and a fricking chainsaw! This was no sex film! This was the set-up for a snuff film. I exhaled deeply. I was fucked.

Scanning the other side of the room, my eyes darting around in search of something I could use to free myself. Then I spotted it on top of the dresser beside me, my daggers resting on my bloodied clothes. Instinctively, I looked down to find he had redressed my wound, and I huffed. Hmm, didn't want me to bleed out before he killed me then!

While he was fiddling with the lighting, his phone rang. He looked over and blew me a kiss, then answered the call.

"Yes, Father," he said. That was him. The man that ran this whole organisation. The man with no name except Daddy.

"She is, father. Would you like me to wait?"

"Yes. I will do. I will be ready for your arrival."

He put down the phone.

Great, his whole family was going to attend this epic snuff film, and I was the main character.

Xander continued to mess about with the lights, then left the room arguing with himself. It was something he used to do when he was stressed... usually when his father was due to visit.

My pulse raced as I peered around the room, desperately searching for a way to escape. That's when I heard them, the cries of the children again. Screams, in fact! They were pleading to be freed from whatever torment that asshole was inflicting on them.

Adrenaline coursed through me as I lay there in absolute fear. I was angry, pissed off in fact, but equally scared at the idea of him coming anywhere near me. Gritting my teeth, I thrashed and tugged at my bindings. I had to act fast if I was going to get any of us out of this alive. I twisted, and thankfully he had given me ample rope to move my legs about, allowing me to position my feet on the bedposts, giving me something hard to push against. I'd seen in the films that people can break their thumbs so they can slide out. That thought was at the back of my mind as a last resort.

This time I managed to get up onto my knees, using the bedposts as leverage. Sweat beaded on my forehead as I pulled with all my might. The bedpost splintered and to my surprise, the bindings loosened, not by much, but just enough to free one of my hands from their clasp.

Sliding free, my heart skipped a beat, and I rushed to free my other wrist and both feet before he came back and stopped me. Taking a deep breath, I jumped off the bed, no longer feeling the pain in my leg. My heart pounded as I grabbed my clothes and daggers, and the children stopped crying. Shit! Has he killed them? That's when his footsteps echoed through the hallway. He was coming back! And he was not alone. The loud shrilling sound of a young child grasped at me; he was dragging one of them back here. Were they to be a star in his snuff film, too?

Throwing on my top and trousers, I grabbed my daggers, and stumbled out of the side door, keeping to the shadows. I recognised the layout of the place and headed down to where the children were likely being held. That's when the shrilling screams stopped, and in its place was the roar of a pissed-off Payne brother heading my way.

Opening the bedroom door, I found all the children huddled in the corner, all but one. I did not have any time to release them, as Xander was hot on my trail. Instead, I took a deep breath, whispered it would be okay and placed my finger to my lips, signalling them to quieten down, as I stood behind the door. Xander's booming footsteps got louder and louder. Right until he burst through the door, spittle foaming at his mouth, fists pummelled and nostrils flaring.

"Where the fuck is she?" he roared. The children began to cry again.

The sound of something being kicked across the floor was my signal to jump out of my hiding place. Daggers raised, eyes wide, I set myself free, launching into the air, both blades poised, impaling him in the back. He cried out, screaming, trying to reach for them, turning to grab me, scrambling to wrap his brutish hands around my neck. I smirked as blood trailed down his back, pooling around his feet.

"You fucking bitch!" he yelled, etching ever closer, wobbling more with every step. Hmm, I think I hit a nerve. He sounds angry. Laughing to myself, I whipped around him, grabbed the blade, and released it as his blood flowed faster. He turned to greet me with the pained face he now wore, so I smirked and grabbed him by his shirt, pulled back the blade and skewered him right through his pride and joy, his manhood.

"There's no way on Earth you'll ever be putting that thing near any of us ever again!"

Pushing him backwards, he stumbled and fell over. The dagger on the back now impaled him further, sticking out of the front of him.

Panting, eyes wide, face pale like a rabbit in the headlights, he whimpered to himself. The effects of blood loss began to take him quicker than I had estimated. So, I did what any self-respecting female would do in this situation. I mounted him. Ripping open his shirt, I took pleasure in drawing back my dagger, positioning it on his chest, and then beginning to carve; showing the world the wolf that he was, and the wolf he always will be.

7

A dark night and a bright morning. Yawning, I raised my sleepy head out of bed, smiling at the good deed I had performed last night. Another asshole was gone, and I saved more innocent children from his brutality. After taking the time to carve the wolf, I explained as best as I could to the young ones, what could have happened if I had never been there. They agreed to keep my secret, allowing me to continue to destroy the devils in this city, and I got to see each of them home.

After I'd called the cops, I had sheltered behind the trees, watching as they walked out, shaking their heads, and delivering the children into the hands of the emergency services. Paramedics checked them over and allowed them to be set free, and sent home to their families again -at least to those that had documented families here in the UK.

The entire experience deserved a celebratory drink. If only I drank more than just the odd cola or lemonade. I laughed to myself. What can I say? Getting drunk isn't my thing. I like to always remain in control, ensuring my safety against the assholes in this city.

So today I was back on shift at the precinct. The usual shower, shit, shave (well legs), and I was ready to go. If only it were that simple. I still had a leg bite I had to redress. I needed to get this thing seen to, but that would give the game away, so I did the next best thing. I bought a bottle of vodka on my way to work and drenched it.

As it was time for work. Monroe met me two blocks over. Apparently, I had forgotten he was picking me up this morning. It's not like I can remember anything nowadays, not with my mind full of my plans for the next big kill.

The car door of the old Volvo opened. "Get in, kid."

"Really, kid… again." Monroe laughed as I got in. He started driving.

"Well, whatever. Have you had breakfast yet?"

"No, why?"

"Good, as we've got another crime scene and I wouldn't want you throwing up all over it."

"Ha de ha!"

"So, what's the crime? Has a bank robbery gone bad? Husband finally shoots his annoying wife? The postal worker went nuts?"

He half-laughed. "Don't knock the postal workers. I'm surprised more of them haven't gone on rage fests. Have you seen what they're paid?"

"Err, no… I take it you have?"

He laughed. "No, well, my brother's son Jayson works there, and he's always pissed off."

Smirking, I waited. He looked at me. "What?" he said, brow furrowed.

"The crime scene?"

"Oh yes, that."

"It's another Wolf."

"Huh? What the same as the wolf from yesterday?"

He smiled and then narrowed his eyes, taking a few seconds to reply. "Yes, the very same. It looks like we have got one mighty pissed off angry ex-girlfriend."

I laughed. "Who was it?"

"Another Payne brother."

I tried to stop myself from smiling, but couldn't. He smirked. "Look, I know you've never been keen on them. But a murder's still a murder and no one deserves to die like that."

I pursed my lips. "Were their kids involved again?"

"Yes."

"Then I beg to differ. He was an asshole."

He laughed. "Clearly."

We pulled up outside of the murderous mansion. A clean, crisp, nauseating place. The type of place I recognised well. My wound ached as I thought about last night's adventure.

Monroe caught me staring. "Everything okay Red?"

"Yeah, it's just so clean."

He smiled. "It's not that clean inside anymore." He knew about my disgust at all things hygienic; I'd told him stories of my life before he found me.

Outside there were two police cars, a forensics van, Harves's car, and an unknown black Bentley.

"Who's here?" I asked, nodding towards the Bentley.

"The new owner."

"New owner? But isn't he the dead guy?"

"No, the victim was his relative."

"Shit, so you're telling me there's one of the Payne family in there?"

"Yes Red, why?" he asked, frowning.

"I, err... oh, no reason," I said, forcing myself to get out of the car. Shit. What if he recognises me? Stefan and Xander did. Shit. Double Shit. Xander phoned his father last night. He would have told him I was there. He was due to turn up for my snuff film! Fuckkkk!

"You coming?" Monroe said, already walking to the main entrance.

"Yeah, just a minute. Got to make a call."

"Sure." He walked in, shaking his head. Okay, so how do I get out of this one? Think damn it think! I pulled my crappy phone out and pretended to be on it. Monroe was waiting at the entrance for me, chatting with a police officer. They parted ways, and the police officer headed my way, handcuffs jangling on his belt. Shit. Does he know?

"Excuse me, mam."

I pretended to say goodbye on my phone call."

"Yes?"

"The detective told me to pass a message on to you." I sighed with relief.

"What is it?"

"He said, and these are his words." I nodded. "To get your scrawny ass inside now."

I smirked. He was an asshole. "Thanks," I replied. He shrugged his shoulders and walked back to the main entrance.

Okay. Get a grip. All I have got to do is stay away from the owner and whatever relative of the Paynes he was. It's not like he's allowed on the crime scene, anyway. Biting my lower lip, I inhaled, held it, and then exhaled quickly. Fuck. My feet started to move.

Moments later, I was at the main entrance, eyeing up every person as I made my way to the bedroom. The Payne guy was nowhere to be seen.

Although I did search every hand of every person, I didn't know, for that broken heart tattoo.

"There you are!" Monroe said, smirking. "I take it you got my message?"

"I did thanks. It was so thoughtful of you."

Harves walked over. "Ah, so the prodigy returns."

"Huh?"

"He's taking the piss," Monroe said. Harves smirked; his old face crooked with it.

I scowled at the old man.

"So, what have we got here?" Monroe said.

"A very dead Xander Payne," I said. He rolled his eyes.

"Ah, there's that witty humour we all know and love," Monroe replied.

"So do we have any leads on the other brother, Stefan?"

"No, nothing concrete," Harves said, watching me.

I nodded and walked over to the corpse. Harves walked out of the room and Monroe followed. "Looks like the same MO." He nodded. "Same wolf, same family…" He nodded again. "Have the kids said anything?"

"No. They are claiming that he blindfolded them." I pinched myself to stop smiling. Clever girls! "But that's the thing. When the officers arrived, they had been untied and there wasn't a blindfold in sight."

"Do you think they did it?" I almost cringed at what I had said.

"No Red, they were too young, didn't have the strength."

"You'd be surprised what strength children have when they need it," I said, thinking back to the girls and me killing Uncle Payne. He sighed, sorrow filling his face as he remembered what I'd told him. He just never knew who the guy was.

"I'm sorry. I forgot."

"That's okay. I will remember for the both of us." He nodded.

"But you were all teenagers back then. These children, some of them, were only six."

"Shit. That's young." I pursed my lips, thinking for a minute. I had to keep playing dumb.

"You don't think…" I said.

He took a deep breath. "I hope not." He knew full well what had happened to me. He knew I was a victim of a trafficking ring. "Jeez, I hope they're not active around here again."

"No, they wouldn't be that stupid." Monroe had kept a file on them ever since he'd found me. He was determined to catch them. The problem was, he knew as well as I, there was no evidence, and with no evidence, it meant no judge or jury would condemn them. So, I gave up telling Monroe anymore. Plus, my way works so much better!

"Right, I think we're done here," he said.

"We've only just got here."

"This is not a good place for you, Red. It's bringing up too many shitty memories."

"Well yeah, but it's my job now."

"Come on, let's wait for forensics to report. We can view the photos and any evidence they collect then." I nodded. I was more than happy to get out of this place if Daddy Payne was lurking around.

He must have heard every one of my final thoughts when I left the room, as right there talking to Harves was one of my old abusers, the Payne relative.

When his eyes gripped mine in a hypnotic trance, I sank back into that spiral of pain, anger, and sorrow. My hands clammed up, teeth gritted, stomach growled, swirled, and twirled, threatening to spill my guts all over the carpet. "Hey Red," Monroe said. I hadn't realised, but he'd stopped before me, staring at me. His hand gripped my arm. I flinched and pulled away. "Red, it's me!"

Holding myself stiff against the wall, Monroe put his hand on my arm again. "Red, are you okay?"

By this time, Harves began walking over. "Ah, is the rookie getting nauseous?" What an asshole!

My abuser was leering at me, looking me up and down, licking his lips. I almost vomited. His feet started to move, and he walked over. "Thank you for helping," he said in his slow, sultry voice. His comment was directed at me.

"I…" my voice failed me, so I nodded, careful not to take my eyes off him.

"Sorry Mr Payne," Harves said. "She's a rookie."

"She looks empathetic to me. After all," he said. "They murdered both my nephews in the last few days." Ah, another uncle. He must know what we did to the last uncle.

Harves nodded, then backed away. Monroe pulled on my arm. I let him. My feet weren't going to move on their own.

Uncle Payne leant closer to me, sniffing against my neck. "So will I see you again... Baby Doll?" he whispered, his arm brushing against mine.

I froze, eyes wide, face pale. "Is everything okay, sir?" an officer asked, walking over.

Monroe was now staring at him. He knew they called me Baby Doll, I'd told him. But did he hear Uncle Payne call me that? He must have. He looked hellishly angry at the uncle. Angry enough that if his back held out, he would put a bullet in him right there and then.

"Red," he said, now yanking my arm. I fell towards him. "Time to go." I absentmindedly nodded and let him pull me the rest of the way out of the mansion.

As I escaped, cool air swept over me, cradling my lost soul in comfort as it brought me back to reality. "You look like you've seen a ghost," he said, helping me to the car.

I shook him off. "I'm okay," I lied. "Must be hungry."

"Hmm." We both got in and silently headed over to the greasy spoon for breakfast. When we arrived, I couldn't face much. Instead, my mind was a mess of convulsions. Had I really seen the man with the broken heart tattoo on his hand? Did he have the tattoo? Had I seen it? My mind was a mess of riddling memories, that I couldn't be sure. I don't think he was my tattooed daddy, just another one of the many that had forced himself on me time and time again.

I stirred the food around on my plate. But had Monroe noticed that? Was he there or had I invented him to cope with my reality? Fuckkkk! I could scream!

"You've hardly touched your food Red, what's going on?"

"I'm not that hungry." Instead, I took a sip of coffee, picking at the bacon on my plate, remembering his wrinkled hands as I pushed it around.

"That's it," he said. "You're off the case."

Now that grabbed my attention. "What? Why?"

"Why? Didn't you see yourself in there?"

"Technically, no, I can't see myself."

"Oh, so now you can be all witty and back to normal! You scared the shit out of me."

"I'm okay, I promise."

"Hmm." Which in Monroe talk meant, I don't believe you.

"Look, whatever's going on, you know you can tell me, right?"

"Yeah, I know." I know I can't. He might arrest me.

"But whatever it is. You need a break; something isn't right, and it doesn't take a world-class detective to see that."

I laughed. "World-class?"

He smirked. "Ah, so you caught that bit then?"

"Couldn't miss the bullshit."

He almost howled with laughter at that point. "Come on, by order of me. You're grounded. No more work for you. Two days off Missie."

"Missie, really."

"I'd go with sweetie, but you told me off for that one last time."

At which point we left the cafe, and he took me home, witty banter continuing along the way.

8

Slithers of tall grass caressed my hands, snaking across my arms as I glided through the vibrant field toward my next target, the last son, Edison Payne.

Alive, yet dead, the field diminished under the ever-darkening light. Sunset corrupted the sky, setting it aflame. Crimson red bled into yellow ochre, with magenta simplifying the edges; and the nature of what was once a silent blue sky began to diminish.

The night became evident with its dark thoughts and monsters stalking the shadows. The power they sought to wield unhinged every one of them; controlling those less fortunate, praying on the small and not-so-mighty. Then there were those, their victims, the trafficked souls of the innocent. The darkened thoughts of man enjoyed toying with every child, corrupting them with their demonic nature. It was rare you would see the traffickers during the daylight. They tend to wilt in the sun; living only in the extravagance and sorrow they grew accustomed to.

There was once a time I pitied them. They were also raised by their father. But when I joined them, they were adults with no chance of rebelling against his name; all three were lost souls, each triggered by their hunger for violence. But now, on this fateful eve, there was only one brother left. I smiled as I continued walking through the tall grass. Two wolves vanquished, perished, and decomposed as we speak.

Now for the final son. This ugly son of a bitch had a thing for the chase. He enjoyed letting his victims go, then chasing and raping them, killing them off… all on camera, of course. I dare not think back to when he first freed me. If their masked Daddy Payne hadn't stopped that hunt, I wouldn't be here now. That was the first and only ever time I heard his proper voice. I find it somewhat comforting, though, to know that there was a real man beneath the act he portrayed.

Walking through this field reminded me of when I was such a young, sweet girl taking my father's hand as we ran together playfully; all whilst my mother picnicked beside our willow tree. To think of them warmed my heart. These were the memories that kept me alive. I can almost feel my father holding my hand, warm to the touch. Family to me, was everything.

It must have been hard for them after their father got sick. He could barely tolerate me even looking at him. He became so frail, fed by a tube. I'm guessing that's why he couldn't fight back when the brothers came that fateful night. I took a deep breath and came to the edge of the woods. It was growing ever so much darker by now. The trees started to deepen their shadows as they danced through the essence of the moonlight.

Biting my lower lip, I fought back the tears as I remembered the last time I saw them. Mother had read me my favourite bedtime story, Red Riding Hood. She was always the hero I wanted to be. Then halfway through, as the wolf hid in the wardrobe to jump out on Grandma, there was a bang downstairs, and the sound of shattered glass. Father was using a cane and Mother darted from my bedside, grabbed the vase in the hall, and disappeared from view. That is when I heard her scream and the bastard brother, Edison, burst into my room licking his lips... just like the wolf did in my story. He pulled me kicking and screaming from my bed. I never saw my mother and father again after that.

To have a daughter ripped away at the hands of another must be a sentence worse than death. I often wondered why they never looked for me.

After all, I was not just missing; They had kidnapped me. I didn't find out the truth until Monroe rescued me that day. After taking us to the hospital, he stayed by my side. I was black and blue with a concussion and three broken ribs.

When he asked who I was, it had taken me a while to remember. All they had ever called me was their Baby Doll. So, when he radioed in, he found out what had happened to my parents. The day they had taken me was also the day they had slaughtered my mother and father as they tried to protect their little girl. After that, the brothers burned our home down, with them inside.

I wondered if this was what happened to the other girls that made it more than a few days. Did they slaughter their families too? Were they treated like cattle taken to the slaughterhouse and disposed of? They must have, as no one ever came looking for us. Either that or some of them were immigrants brought in from the war abroad; never documented, never lost.

Walking through the woods, I made sure I made little to no noise, knowing full well Edison and his group of hunters would be setting up nearby.

Some part of me likes to think about what happens after I've destroyed the whole family. I often wonder if there is such a thing as a life outside the wall. My mind dictates would I ever find someone to love me, will I have a child, can I mother a baby in this broken body? It is perhaps a pipe dream, but could it be possible that one I will find a man I love and trust? One I can let near me, allow him to touch me in a way that doesn't make me flinch, scream or cry?

But I know, I know that even after the Payne family is dead and buried, there will be others. Humanity is evil, there is too much darkness to hope I can ever live in such a future. I wish I could rely on the sole purpose of the law, to protect and serve. But the legal system is too busy reacting to the aftermath of the crime, than being proactive and taking these bastards down before they murder someone else.

It is tough for them though. These criminals are hardened. They're clever, never showing their face on camera, showing no tattoos that could identify them. The videos concentrated mainly on the children and the distress that they endured.

I shudder to think about it. But then, building a brick wall around my past has been the only way I've survived these last years.

My therapist does not seem to think so. She said we needed to delve into the darkness, but it would kill me all over again. I know I'm not ready for that. Why would I ever want to relive the moments that I'm trying so hard to put behind me? It may not be healthy, but it's my life, and this is how I've learned to live with it.

Passing from tree to tree, I watched my every step. There were fallen branches that threatened to snap and give away my position, but with a little patience, I managed to bypass every one of them; so, I continued.

It was obvious that Edison was a sick bastard. He had taken the trivial beauty of sport to a sadistic, deadly level. This cat-and-mouse game would end in catastrophe, with all the little mice being eaten by the fat, sluggish cat.

I would say it should be easy to outrun the weighty thuggish asshole. But it wasn't him I had to worry about. It was the other men he had around him; his paying customers, gleaning for the opportunity to hunt down a child and do whatever they wanted with them. This wasn't a fun game as they once sold it to us as… no, this was a sport, and the prize was a quick death, if you were lucky.

I crept up on the group of five masked men loading their shotguns and shining their blades. One older gentleman carried an axe, his wrinkled hands grasping the handle with strained fingers. The other two were laughing at the baseball bats they had with them, pretending to hit each other, feigning death. This pair creeped me out. They had the same joker masks on, with flamboyant clothing and no care for anything or anyone. Especially as one of them swung his bat too far, hitting the old guy on the back. That started a brawl, broken apart by Edison and another masked character I couldn't quite make out.

Behind them were a small group of barefoot children, five of them, and all of them of various ages. They were all young girls, dressed in shimmering white nightgowns. The eldest looked barely sixteen by the looks of it, whereas the others I dread to think how old they were! The two youngest clung to each other, with the older girl standing in front of them as if she was protecting them from some unknown force.

I checked my watch and shook my head, taking a deep breath. If the rules were the same, the game would start soon. Biting my lip, I sunk back behind the tree. With so many of them, I would barely have a chance to escape with my life, let alone stop the mass slaughter that was about to happen.

Watching, I waited. Tonight would be a test of both my patience and my skills. I exhaled long and hard. These rich bastards are paying for this 'privilege!' not only that, they enjoy inflicting harm on others, on what I would consider the innocent and the pure. Even after living this life for so long, it still can shock me.

Focusing on the target, I watched his every move. He was the reason I was here. I know there are five girls there that need saving, and I will try to… shit, I had to try to. But he was the reason I'd come.

Gritting my teeth, I stared down at my blades, all shiny and shimmering in the moonlit sky. Was it disturbing that I looked forward to seeing Edison's crimson blood coat the surface? Gliding down the hilt, and smothering my delicate, yet worn hands, which were tired from the traumatic life I led?

"Pack it in, lads!" Edison shouted, scolding the two jokers. They started sniggering. Jeez, how old are they? I growled under my breath. I expect they are both from snobbish families that own half of this city. Too much money and makes no sense. It's a dangerous combination. He climbed onto a large rock, bowed and welcomed his 'hunters.' "Tonight is the night you become men!" he yelled. The old guy groaned, shifting his axe to his other shoulder.

"The rules are," he yelled. "There are no rules!" Edison raised his hands high and all the men cheered. "We will release the girls and give them a ten-minute head start. After that, the night is your own. Chase, catch, fuck, and kill, in any which way you please!" The two young jokers cheered again, pretending to fuck the air, blowing kisses to the girls.

The eldest girl pushed the children back, whispering silent words, trying to comfort them.

"Is everyone ready?" he yelled, glaring at the children, horn poised and ready. "Ready... Steady... Go!" The eldest cried out, grabbed the two young ones, and ran. The other two girls followed, running as fast as their little legs could carry them.

The horn sounded loud and clear; deafened only by the pitter-patter of children running through the woods, their heavy breaths and strangled cries echoing through the forest. The game had started and by the look on the last son's face; I was soon to be a part of it.

9

Shit. Eyes fixated on me. Mouth snarling in anger, Edison waved his hand forward and signalled the start of the hunt. The two jokers whooped and hollered with glee as they charged forward with their baseball bats at the ready. The old man grumbled, taking a slow pace but with so much determination that it sent shivers down my spine. Last but not least was the dark figure, unseen, yet he seemed to be menacingly hot on my tail. At least if they were chasing me, they weren't gunning for the children! Without a second thought, the jokers turned off the trail, disappearing into the darkness of the forest.

"We're coming for you!" they shouted. Screaming echoed through the darkness, as the children ran and fled.

I ran with all I had, dodging trees, branches, streams, and rocks as I made my escape. The darkness hindered me more than it did the men chasing me; they seemed to know this terrain like the back of their hands. I could feel their eyes on my every move, tracking me like prey in the wild.

Howling winds began tearing through the leaves, pushing me further from danger. But no matter how fast I ran, I could still hear their footsteps getting closer and closer -echoing within my eardrums like gunshots.

Adrenaline coursed through my veins, my lungs burning up from the lack of air, and my heart thumped against my chest like a drum. All I could hear were the heavy steps of Edison as he huffed and puffed, giving chase. The worrying thing was, I could no longer hear the footsteps of the other men. Where were they?

I ran until exhaustion threatened to render me useless, but I kept going when suddenly something caught my attention... A glimmering light ahead pierced through the darkness. The shimmer of an axe severed the air, catching my attention for a split second, followed by the infernal cry of a young child. Was I too late? Anger coursed through my veins. I hadn't the time for this merciless pursuit.

Fists pummelled, I pulled out my blades, turned around and caught Edison mid-run. Resistance pulled at the blade as it penetrated his skin, slicing his stomach. Pressure shot through my arm and his villainous blood tinged the surface of the blade. He yelped, gurgling obscene remarks, as if that would give him some kind of extra strength to their already powerful strides.

Wounded and slowed to a snail's pace, I left him, trailing blood over the cold, damp forest floor. He can wait. They can't. So, I ran. I sprinted faster than ever before, guided by the still-distant sound of a helpless child's cries. I chased after them, weaving in and out of trees as I went. It felt like a race against time; every second that passed brought me closer and closer to who knows what kind of horror she was facing.

Then something powerful overtook me; an immense surge of energy suddenly invigorated my body, bringing hope that I could make it in time. My mind raced, and thoughts spilt into action as my fingers gripped around the hilt of each blade. Taking one last leap forward, I pounced, raising my blade above my head, aiming right between his shoulder blades, the exact place I knew he could never reach. As I landed, the sharpened point leapt through him, piercing his skin, as he let out a howl in the darkness, dropping the heavy axe, and letting it land before his feet.

The child was cowering in fear, arms shielding her face from the impending danger. It seemed like time had stopped completely. But seconds later, I emerged victorious. Adrenaline coursed through my veins as I wrenched the old guy away from the girl's fragile figure. He would have been able to chop me up like firewood had I not got the drop on him. I was lucky, plain and simple, but would I always be?

The forest winds stirred, as the frightened young girl cowered before me, hiding behind her dirtied hands. What was once a white nightgown was now muddy and torn. "It's okay," I whispered. She nodded slowly, wiping the dirt and tears from her face. The gargling man with the axe was now as dead as a doornail, so I took to imprinting my boot on his back and yanking my blade free. Good shot, I thought, looking down at where the blade had pierced. Looks like it hit the artery. Admiring my handy work, I picked up the axe and gave it to the girl. It was way too big for her! "How old are you?" I asked, curiosity getting the better of me.

"I am six, but nearly seven. My papa says I am seven next Tuesday."

Oh, bless her heart. "Well, six, nearly seven. I have a gift for you." She nodded, her sorrowful eyes brightened and a faint smile appeared on her little lips. "You see this blade here?" I pulled out my spare blade, wiped the blood off, and handed it to her. She instinctively went to touch the shiny steel. "Oh no, sweet girl, don't put your fingers there. You'll slice them off!" So, she dropped it instead.

I half-laughed, picking it up. "Look, you hold it here." I showed her how to hold the blade and where on the body to stab should she need to. The gut was the easiest place for her. She wasn't tall enough to hit anything higher. Plus, it's usually fatty, and the skin is easier to get through. She took the blade from me.

"But remember, always keep the shiny part away from yourself, and only pull it out if one of the nasty men catches you." She nodded again. "Okay, do you have somewhere to hide?" I asked. Knowing full well I would get her killed if she tailed along beside me. She looked around and saw a thicket of brambles. A painful place, but one they'd never look in. So, I helped her inside, holding back the brambles so she could find a gap to sit in. "Okay, little one. I will come and get you when it's safe to." She nodded, her lower lip twitching. "Stay there, no matter what you hear. You stay there and be as quiet as a mouse." I waited for a response, but there was none. "Okay?"

"Okay..." she said, tears starting to pool around her chin.

I pulled her in for one last hug and did something I'd never done before. "I'm called... Red," I said. She nodded and smiled.

"I'm Mia."

Kissing her forehead, I turned away, covered her with brambles and wiped the tear from my eye, praying she would survive the night.

Walking through the forest, I listened as the trees swayed, dancing under the moonlight, unaware of the horror wrapped within their home. That horror came to light as streams of torch lights pierced the darkness, bringing with them the fear of children's screams. Damn it! They've caught another! Running as fast as I could, I headed towards the girl's cries. There were two, by the sounds of it, one a higher pitch than the other.

Jumping over mounds of dirt, broken branches, and what was once a graveyard of many girls before us, I made my way to a thicket with an opening in the dense trees. Two young girls sat huddled together, cowering in the centre. Around them, the two jokers danced, swinging their baseball bats, which were already covered in blood.

Swirling and twirling their riddle some bodies around the girls, they laughed and drooled, kicking out at something on the floor. A dark mass became their number one target, giving the children a chance to up and run until their little legs could run no more.

I waved at the girls, trying to divert their attention away from the monstrous masked fiends and onto me. But it was no use. No matter how much I waved, nothing would make them take their eyes off the beasts before them.

The squelching sounds of the bloodied mass on the floor began to cough and splutter. Shit! It was another girl. I'd been sitting here watching them kick, beat, and pummel the poor girl, almost to death, without even knowing it.

Fuck this. Running free from the clearing, I raised the axe, roaring in anguish at the broken older girl lying on the floor. They had caused the poor girl's body to shatter. It was covered with bruises that swelled her face so much that her right eye was beyond repair. With a ripped nightdress, I could see that one of her legs was shorter, twisted in an unnatural direction. It took everything I had not to drop the axe and vomit everywhere. Her one eye pleaded with me as she saw me run towards her, axe raised. The pain she must have felt was unbearable and no matter how hard I fought; she would not survive another few minutes. So, I did the only thing I could do in this horrible situation. I slammed the axe onto her neck, giving her a clean death.

The jokers jumped backwards, yelping. "What the fuck!" the shorter one said. "She was our kill!" He turned around and saw me.

"Hey where's your mask?" the other said.

"You weren't with us." The shorter one said. "Where'd you get the axe?"

I stepped back, hand on my blade, axe still embedded in the ground.

The taller one laughed like a hyena. "If she ain't with us, she's one of them."

The shorter one nodded, and they both raised their bats high, ready to end my life right there and then. The taller one tried, but as I avoided his swing, he lost his footing and went down in a heap on the ground.

The other swung high, and I ducked, forcing my body forward and rugby-tackled the shorter sicko to the floor. The blade pierced his skin. Blood flowed freely from his abdomen. But in his eyes, as he cried out yelping, I saw the image of his brother swinging his bat high above my head. In an instant I'd rolled free out of the way, watching as his brother's action crushed the bat down on his head. Blood and brain matter spewed into the air like an explosion of confetti at a funeral.

The taller one cried out, dropping his bat as he fell, kneeling in the bloody brains of his twin brother. He spat out the word "WHY!" The anger, pain, and devastation of that connection he'd lost, and the guilt would forever eat him from the inside out.

It took me a moment to right myself and wipe off the brain matter that coated my face. Even though it was another monster from the streets of this city, this didn't make me feel as accomplished.

Plus, I'd be picking out his brain from my hair for weeks!

"YOU FUCKING BITCH!" the remaining Joker screamed, grabbing his bat and swinging it wildly. Jeez! He was pissed. I shot backwards, merely escaping him. He kept coming, furiously coating his body, electrifying his veins, until it left no humanity within him.

The funny thing is, he wasn't about to be the source of my pain, nor was the tree stump I butted up against. With the dagger poised ready for the next attack, I failed to notice the obvious elephant in the room. It was that elephant that smacked me over the head, way before the Joker ever could. That elephant was the one that bought twinkling stars into my field of vision. Pain as it radiated through me, black curtains drew over my eyes, and an endless, suffocating sleep took hold as I collapsed to the floor unconscious.

10

Eyelids fluttering, grazed by the earthy smell, corrupted by the absence of light, I stretched. Palms reached out, scraping against crumbling earth, slithering over roots as they wound their way up and over my body. What the hell?

I sat up, or at least attempted to, banging my head on the solid planks above me, caging me inside, providing the very coffin I was going to die in. Darkness. The solid blankness of realism. It's that breathless state when your heart skips a beat, all colour drains from your body and your mind screams out as you freeze in a state of shock.

Static pressure engulfed me, and my stiffened frame begged me to stop, but nothing came of my mind's cries. Nothing appeared to help, as my vocal cords shrilled and screamed. I was lost down here and no one or nothing would ever halt the pure desperation that flowed through my veins. I was a corpse still breathing, but considering the lack of air, it wouldn't be long before that seized to exist too.

Clawing at the planks of wood, my nails shattered, embedding their bloody bodies in the ground that would swallow them whole. It was useless to keep trying, to beg for a god when there was none.

I had lived a shallow life of despair and preyed on every deity to be set free before now, but no one and nothing ever came, except for Monroe.

Taking a deep breath, I fumbled in my front pocket for my phone. That was gone, too. Is it possible, though, was there any glimpse of hope that he could have followed me, maybe… would even try to find me? He would see the fresh dirt. I bit my lower lip. But would he? It's dark outside. Would he see my grave before the sun rose, and all the air suffocated my poor human lungs? I sighed. Then told myself off for sighing. If there was any chance of surviving this, I need to conserve as much oxygen as I could, and sighing certainly would not help the situation.

Drawing back my bloody fingertips, I began to dig. Dry dirt crumbled in, blissfully unaware of the trauma it caused my air supply. I coughed. Winced, then coughed again. Fists pummelled; teeth gritted, I kicked out at the sodding planks with all my might. I would rather be crushed under this mud pile than lay here awaiting my death! So, I kicked again, then some more and more. Mud shifted, planks moved, and the ground above me rumbled. Someone's got to notice that! But after a while, I realised they hadn't.

Sorrow grabbed my gut and crushed it. I don't know what else to do. Tears choked back in my throat, pooling around my eyes, falling, and resting on the hard surface I lay on. Slowly but surely, I unclenched my hands, relaxing my aching body and letting the tears absorb into my soul. Perhaps this is the way I go. Maybe for all the bloodshed I've caused, this is a justified ending to my miserable life? So, with a quivering lip, I soothed myself to sleep, wrapping my arms around myself and crying until no tears would escape me no more.

It was a nightmare, an evil dream to perplex and destroy the day ahead of you. I opened my eyes, expecting the mild sunrise through the crack of my shredded curtains, but nothing was far from the truth. The nightmare was, nor would it be ever a dream. It was reality, and as I coughed, freeing my clogged throat, I realised that the air had dwindled to a near standstill in my sleep.

This was it. The darkness had swallowed me whole and spat out my mortal soul, severing my body under the ground and trapping me for an eternity. An infinite amount of time, perhaps, seen as time no longer existed down here. No, in fact, it could have been days, weeks, months or years, not bare minutes, or hours until my strangled suffocation. It didn't matter which way was up or which way was down. My heart ruptured, leaking into the abyss surrounding me.

It reminds me of the night sky, without the stars. A weightless body floating freely into space, transcending gravity into another world entirely. Perhaps I was.

Slow, hardened breaths forced in and out of me. Rough, thick air nestled inside my windpipe, restricting the space, and allowing no more than a slow trickle of oxygen into my lungs. There was little to nothing left. My body stiffened, my hands clawed at my throat, my feet kicked out, and my eyes bulged. This was it. It was time. Face bloated.

My heart pounded, and my body began to seize. Pain lessened. My heart slowed, and I eased into the coffin one beat at a time. My eyelids fluttered, my body was weightless, and peace blessed me for the last time.

The light was bright. I'd never imagined it to be this bright, except there wasn't a tunnel, nor a shiny halo-headed Angel there to show me the way. But then at least there wasn't fire, a demon or damnation. No, this light blinded me, moving like a torchlight swaying above as the numbness of my body began to creep back to feeling. Coughing and spluttering. It felt like I'd smoked a whole cigarette shop of tobacco as my chest burned, roaring with pain. Was I alive? Heaven shouldn't hurt this much... should it?

The figure above swayed the torchlight up and over my body, watching as I clambered up to sit in the corner of my coffin, covering my eyes from the brightness. Who was it? Was I safe here?

I was about as safe as a lowly girl could be in a coffin on a darkened night.

Crouching down, the darkened man reached out to me, offering his hand as a gesture of help in this somewhat dire situation. I bit my lower lip. Damn it! I have no choice! I was on my way to the good stuff a few seconds ago. It's not like this creep can make my life any worse.

As I took his hand, his skin wrapped over my fingertips, moving and urging me to be set free. Dazed from the light, I blinked twice to make out his face. Yes, that mat of a hairstyle, the greying moustache framing his distant lips. Monroe.

But his eyes, hard, brown, darkened eyes. Those were different. They told a tale, a twisted, gruesome fairy tale of a young girl in a red cloak running through the woods chased by the hungry evil wolf. I gulped back bile as I saw through the mask, into the parts of him he'd shadowed from the rest of the world. And as he gripped my hand, he never pulled, never urged me up into his arms.

He held me there, glaring down at me. His figure darkened, wearing nothing but black.

Stunned to silence, my throat strangled by the air that suffocated me, I yelped out. That Cheshire cat grin, and those eyes, those forgotten, plagued eyes. They burrowed into your soul, laid bare in my trauma, and as the darkness became reality, as did the memories. The memory of him comforting me after a desperate bedtime session. The pain as he soothed away my sorrow, his face always masked, but his eyes cradled me to the grave.

In the distance, the screams of young girls echoed through the night. A joker cackled, and the moonlight dimmed as the wolf stepped closer, leaning down. I looked at the hand that bore mine and saw remnants of skin hanging free from it, revealing the broken heart tattoo as he jumped in the coffin on top of me and scowled, speaking the only words that made sense anymore.

"Welcome home, Baby Doll."

OTHER BOOKS BY ANNALEE

The Resurgence series:
The Heart of the Phoenix
The Rise of the Vampire King
The Fall of the Immortals
The Birth of Darkness

The Fire Wolf Prophecies:
Crimson Bride
Crimson Army

The Shop Series:
Stake Sandwich
The Devil Made Me Do It
Strawberry Daiquiri Desire

The Celestial Rose Series:
Eternal Entity
Eternal Creation
Eternal Devastation
Eternal Ending

Gruesome Fairy Tales:

Gretel

Hansel

Red

Wolf (Coming Soon)

AUTHOR'S NOTE

Thank you for reading Red, I hope you enjoyed the story! I always appreciate your feedback and would really be grateful if you could leave me a review on Amazon– just a few words makes all the difference!

As with all authors, reviews mean the world to me. It keeps me going, helps me strengthen my writing style and help's this story become a success.

CONNECT WITH ANNALEE

Join Annalee on social media. She is regularly posting videos and updates for her next books on TikTok and Facebook.

Join Annalee in her Facebook group:

Annalee Adams Bookworms & Bibliophiles.

Also, subscribe to Annalee's newsletter through her website - for free books, sales, sneak previews and much more.

Subscribe at www.AnnaleeAdams.biz

TikTok: @author_annaleeadams

Website: www.AnnaleeAdams.biz

Email: AuthorAnnaleeAdams@gmail.com

Facebook:

https://www.facebook.com/authorannaleeadams/

ABOUT ANNALEE

Annalee Adams was born in Ashby de la Zouch, England. Annalee spent much of her childhood engrossed in fictional stories. Starting with teenage point horror stories and moving on up to the works of Stephen King and Dean Koontz. However, her all-time favourite book is Lewis Carroll's, Alice in Wonderland.

Annalee lives in the UK with her supportive husband, two fantastic children, little dog, and kitten. She's a lover of long walks on the beach, strong cups of tea and reading a good book by candlelight.

Printed in Great Britain
by Amazon

42889487R00078